FOREST
OF
MYSTICAL
CREATURES
Beyond The Brambles

M.R. MYERS
PICTURES BY JEANNETTE ROSS

Fulton Books, Inc.
Meadville, PA

Published by Fulton Books 2021

ISBN 978-1-63710-127-8 (paperback)
ISBN 978-1-63985-158-4 (hardcover)
ISBN 978-1-63710-128-5 (digital)

Printed in the United States of America

Once upon a time in a far-off land deep in the woods where not one human soul had ever stepped, there was a grand fairy kingdom that existed. High in the treetops, there were structures of all kinds—small houses, large houses, and shops up and down the branches. All were connected by an intricate web of rope ladders and bridges. In the center of all this magnificence stood the oldest and tallest tree. Within this tree, the royal family lived. The king and the queen made everything good and happy for all who lived in their kingdom. They had three children—the eldest, Princess Obryn, who had begun her intensive training to become queen when the time came; the middle child, Prince James; and the youngest, Princess Charlotte.

The two youngest were and had always been a handful for the king and queen, constantly causing a ruckus about the kingdom. Charlotte was the schemer of the two, and James went along because he loved the sense of adventure. The thing was James was also quite clumsy, one might say, always running into things or objects and breaking them when he was around. By no fault of his own, it was as if disaster simply followed him wherever he went. So inevitably, the two children would be caught doing whatever scheme Charlotte had cooked up that day.

Now today, Charlotte had decided it would be a fun game to race through the swarm of wild dragonflies as fast as possible without bumping into one of them. Of course, James wanted to join in on the fun; and without fail, a falling leaf fell right into his face, causing him to go blind just long enough that he flew face-to-face into several dragonflies at a time. This made the dragonflies so flustered that they began buzzing every which way throughout the kingdom, knocking down the booths set up for the market that day. There was food and goods going in all directions. When the last dragonfly had gone, there in the middle of the mess were James and Charlotte.

That night, James and Charlotte had to answer to the king and queen, who were greatly disappointed in their children's actions. They decided that for the next three days, James and Charlotte would have to stay within the palace walls. Neither one of the children were happy about this punishment. Both of them cried themselves to sleep that night with Charlotte arguing how it was unfair. Obryn was thankful that her room was in a different branch of the palace, especially on nights such as this when the whining and crying would go on and on.

The next day, James and Charlotte spent all morning moping about the palace until their mother sent them to the kitchen to help prepare the evening's meal. The kitchen staff knew the children well and had the perfect job for them. So Charlotte could put to use some of her energy and James could be safe from dropping a pot of soup, they sent the two out to gather berries for a freshly baked pie for dessert and muffins for the following morning. The children accepted the task with smiling faces, for they were glad to be freed from the solid confines of the old tree's walls.

The place where the berries grew was not within the kingdom's perimeter but just beyond the other side. It was a clearing that went far and wide, bush after bush, covered with plump, luscious berries of every color and taste. There are sweet berries, bitter berries, sourberries, and tart berries. There are red berries, blueberries, and blackberries. This field of berries was widely known throughout the land. Fairies would come from faraway places because they had heard that there was only one place that had the best berries one would ever taste. However, there was a magic veil that surrounded the berries. It could only be seen by those touched by the fairy world. To all others, the clearing and the berries were merely nonexistent. The berries were also hidden from the fairy folk who had been punished by the king and queen until which time their punishment was lifted. This fact was the one overlooked by the kitchen staff this afternoon when they sent Charlotte and James to their task.

Charlotte had flown as fast as she could from the old tree with James two lengths behind, whining loudly for Charlotte to slow down and wait. In his attempt to fly close to Charlotte, James misjudged a corner and landed feet in the air inside a patch of dead brush that had culled from the trees. It was this incident alone that would change the royal children's afternoon from a pleasant task to an uninvited adventure. They were not aware, nor noticed that they had reached the edge of the kingdom and the beginning of the great veil.

After James was untangled from the brush and his wings straightened, the two continued their flight toward a berry field they would never find, for it was hidden from their sight until their punishment was lifted by their parents.

They had flown on for some time when James mentioned to Charlotte that they might possibly be lost. At first, Charlotte did not listen, actively ignoring James with his concerns. She insisted they were going the right way and they would be there soon.

The air got a chill, and the sun began to dull. With this, Charlotte turned to James with a rather worried look upon her face.

James knew this look quite well and did not like it one bit. This was the look Charlotte had when she realized she was wrong and should have listened to James. As soon as James made eye contact, Charlotte crumpled to the ground in a sobbing mess. James tried to comfort her, but it was no use. Charlotte was afraid of the dark. She was scared to go into a dark room in her own tree where things were familiar, never mind the thought of being lost in the forest at night and outside the protection of the kingdom's walls. With this thought, James crumpled beside Charlotte, hugging her but not crying in an attempt to stay strong for his little sister.

As the air grew chillier and the sun grew dimmer, James continued to reassure Charlotte that somebody from the kingdom would come along soon to collect them and bring them safely home. What the royal children did not realize was that when James had crashed into the brush earlier that day, he had flown right into the invisible veil that protects the field of berries. By doing so, the veil reacted by displacing the potential intruders far from the kingdom walls and the field. The place where they were now was one where even the bravest of their father's warriors did not travel. This was the place of the mystical creatures.

Hours had passed, the sun had almost set, and James and Charlotte had come to terms that they would camp there for the night. James built a shelter while Charlotte started a fire. Halfway through their dinner, which was the lunch they had packed but never ate, there was a rustling in the bushes. Charlotte jumped across the fire and behind James, knocking him off-balance, sending the bucket of water sitting beside him onto the fire, putting the fire out. Now shivering in the darkness, the rustling of the bushes got louder and closer. Then...it stopped. Both James and Charlotte instantly held their breath in hopes it would make them disappear.

It seemed like forever had passed. Charlotte slowly let her breath out, making as little noise as possible. She had perfected this skill from doing it so often at home in her room at night when she got frightened. James, on the other hand, had held his breath slightly too long, losing control of his lungs and gasping loudly for air. From the darkness just beyond the fire circle, they heard a soft whisper.

"Hello?"

James and Charlotte did not answer, but again came a soft whisper.

"Hello? Who hides in the darkness with no name to themselves?"

Both James and Charlotte huddled together, still as stone, with no words to be said. They heard the creature shuffling about in an attempt to navigate around the hot coals still barely aglow from the bucket disaster just moments before. James determined the creature was upright and moved on two legs, but it was Charlotte who pinpointed the fact that the feet were not of fairy folk but indeed that of cloven hooves. This realization frightened them both, for this fact alone made their whereabouts a reality to them. They now knew they had reached the Forest of Mystical Creatures. All they knew of this land were what they heard in children's stories told around the campfires by travelers passing through.

Their eyes had now adjusted to the darkness, and what they saw before them made the pair of them wide-eyed and slack-jawed. Right before their very noses stood a fawn, a creature with legs of a goat and torso, arms and head of a human. He had the look of a young boy. He had a head of blond with big blue eyes that seemed to twinkle despite the lack of light. The part of him that was goat was that of a gray fur, shiny and sleek as if freshly bathed.

For a third time, the fawn attempted to communicate. "Hello? I am Jacob. What names do you call yourselves, please?"

James, trying to collect himself, wondering whether he had fallen asleep and was now dreaming, spoke next, first with a stutter. "I-I-I am J-J-James of the Crawdorf Clan, son of King Larcs."

"Ahh," replied Jacob, "you are far from home, yes? You are lost then, aye?"

This last comment was said with a mischievous half-smile from the fawn.

A memory sparked within Charlotte just then of the stories told of these creatures. They are known for their trickery upon the unsuspecting but can be ultimately loyal to those they befriend. All in all, there is no telling for sure, leaving a bit of doubt with whoever may come across one of these creatures. With this flicker of memory, Charlotte whispered a warning to James.

Jacob, being close enough now to see both James and Charlotte clearly, saw the change of expression on James's face and immediately cut in. "No, no, I assure you I mean no harm through trickery or mischievousness. I see that the two of you are pure of heart and mean no harm toward me. I would like to help you find your way as you are young and far from home. These woods can be dangerous to the inexperienced."

Charlotte, still weary, clung to her brother's side, speechless.

Not seeing an alternative and being quite frightened at the thought of being alone in the woods, James accepted Jacob's offer.

Pleased by this, Jacob began rebuilding the fire with dry branches lying about the camp. "You must sleep now, for we have a long journey ahead of us yet," said Jacob as he gestured James and Charlotte toward a patch of fresh green moss.

James and Charlotte looked at the spot with amazement and wonder. They both knew this lime-green patch was certainly not there when they had set up camp just a few hours before.

Jacob just smiled his mischievous smile and replied, "Magical things happen in these parts. Some for the good"—pointing toward the newly grown crop of moss— "and some for the evil." As if on cue, there was a high-pitched screech not so far off through the trees. The three all looked at one another, James and Charlotte with terrified, colorless faces and Jacob with a face of majestic bravery that hid his slight discomfort that was just below the surface.

"Do not worry, my new friends, for I will stay awake through the night and assure you your safety. We, mystical folk, do not need sleep to function. But it is something we do to pass the hours."

By this time, Jacob had gotten the fire up and running. James and Charlotte were snuggled together on their patch of moss well on their way to a dreamless sleep. That night, Jacob did as he said—keeping the fire alive and warm while watching over the young royal children as they slept to rejuvenate their small selves.

The next morning, the three friends set off on their journey back to the kingdom just as the sun rose over the horizon. They traveled through the morning and into the late afternoon, snacking on nuts and tree roots. Charlotte was enjoying her surroundings, picking exotic flowers and herbs she had never encountered within the boundaries of her home. James walked in front alongside Jacob, engaged in friendly conversation with his newfound companion. Jacob walked along, purposefully listening to James's stories. He occasionally pulled James out of the way of a tree that happened to be growing in his path or the hump of a root popped above the surface to trip the nonobservant traveler.

They came upon a riverbank where they decided to stop for a drink. Jacob looked up at the sky, stretched his arms out wide and took in a deep breath of fresh forest air. The sun showed it was tired and would be setting within two hours' time. Three brightly colored birds flew over, off on their own adventure. With this, Jacob remembered he had travel companions of his own. He wasn't used to being with anyone but himself. Jacob turned to see James resting with his eyes closed, leaning up against a tree trunk, and Charlotte sitting in the tall grass by the bank, wearing a head wreath of assorted wildflowers she had picked.

"Here is a place to rest your heads for the night. Danger lurks not far in the darkness of the sun."

A slight shiver ran down the back of James from this comment by Jacob. He looked over to his sister, who was merrily weaving her flower crown. "Good, she didn't hear," said James to himself in a whisper under his breath. "Charlotte, we are camping here for the night. You can go collect the firewood we will need. Jacob will build a cover since it smells as if it will rain. I am going fishing so we can eat some hot dinner."

Off they went, each to their own task. Jacob collected the largest of the fallen branches and began to crisscross them, creating a teepee-type structure. Charlotte frolicked through the lightly wooded area, gathering little sticks and twigs that would keep them warm through the night. James had warned her not to go so far that she could no longer see Jacob and their shelter. James headed downstream to a river pool they had passed not too long before they had stopped to rest. He had made note of the jumping fish, hoping he would be skilled enough to catch a few fish for a plentiful dinner.

Jacob had finished the shelter with the opening facing where the fire would be. Charlotte had made a few trips by this time, stacking the wood neatly into piles ranging in size and thickness of the sticks. She had gone to get her final batch but seemed to have been gone too long for Jacob's comfort. As if the forest had heard Jacob's worried thoughts, he heard a series of whistling noises followed by a sudden thunk right by his left ear—an arrow! Jacob knew the danger that followed, for the arrow that had merely missed his ear belonged to the Solero Clan, a clan of centaurs that scoured the mystical land to rid it of true evil.

Without a second thought, he ran to the river pool to get James. As Jacob approached, he saw that James was wrestling with a baby mongrel fish and falling flat on his bottom into the water, losing the battle, becoming soaked from head to toe. Jacob was breathless, unable to call out to James. However, as James trudged through the water, wiping it from his face, he saw the panic in Jacob's expression and the absence of his sister.

At that moment, James's heart leaped into his throat as he scrambled toward the shore. Tripping on a couple of slippery rocks then running into a floating log, James finally made it to Jacob. Through breathless gasps and sputtering water, the boys managed a message between one another that sounded like gibberish.

"Charwhisarrow?"

They ran back to camp. Jacob had gone for James, for he knew that if true evil was near, Charlotte had most likely already found it. James would need Jacob in order to have any chance of surviving if it were to encounter them.

Meanwhile, Charlotte picked up the last piece of wood that would possibly fit into her tiny arms. She was whistling a merry tune of an old fairy folk song the queen has sung to her every night since she was born.

> The mighty warriors fight 'gainst evil
> To prevent any upheaval
> For they are tried and true
> For they are tried and true
> All the young ladies fare-thee-well
> And hope there is a wedding bell

For they are tried and true
For they are tried and true...

She was lost in her own world and did not realize the accompaniment whistling she heard was not in her head but in fact arrows flying overhead and on either side of her.

It was the rumbling of the earth that brought Charlotte out of her wistful trance. As she looked up, she was shot back into her reality. She was lost in the Forest of the Mystical Creatures with no real direction on how to get home. Now the ground was shaking as she fought to keep her balance, and there was a black shadow of a blur dodging through the trees, coming straight for her. Not too far behind was a whole band of centaurs rapidly sending arrows through the air in hopes of hindering the progress of the ever-accelerating black shadow. Charlotte was frozen with fear and "awe." She dropped her bundle of carefully selected firewood but could not manage to move her feet. They were glued to the ground just like the time she had laid adhesive on the ground in attempts to capture a wild, squirmy worm but instead caught herself because she had forgotten about her own trap. However, when that happened, she did not have the Black Shadow of evil sprinting toward her with a wild band of battle-enraged centaurs close behind. She felt faint, and as her vision faded to black, she felt a weightlessness to her body as if she was being lifted straight up into the air directly from the spot she stood.

The skies were faintly starlit when she finally woke. She felt warm and comfortable, though dazed. Charlotte neither knew where she was nor how she had arrived. As her senses came to, she became aware of the wool blanket she was wrapped in and the warmth of the small fire her body lay beside. The air had a smell that was not simply firewood.

What was it? Charlotte wondered. Then she heard voices, not one or two but several— first, a deep voice, assuringly male, then others that sounded as if they belonged to both women and children. At this point, Charlotte still had not dared to move. Her back was turned to the fire as well as the voices. As she lay there listening, she wondered why she struggled with understanding the conversation among the voices around her and suddenly realized the words being spoken were of the old language, all but extinct within the kingdom. However, as a member of the royal family, she was required to study it in school. With this final thought, Charlotte drifted back to sleep.

Jacob and James headed out of the camp in the direction Charlotte had gone for wood. They did not have to travel far before they found arrows sticking into the trees which was—an obvious indicator that the Solero Clan had been through the area. James started to feel ill, then he saw the disheveled pile of assorted sticks and lost his stomach in the nearest bush.

"No time to empty oneself, Sir James, for we must hurry. These arrows of the Solero Clan indicate they are hunting, and it is not food they are after. The Solero Clan is known throughout this land to be the sole hunters of the Black Shadow of Evil."

James had heard of the Black Shadow of Evil, though, and had thought it to be just another tale told by the elders of the kingdom in order to scare the youth into obedience. With the realization that this evil creature that haunted every child's dreams was, in fact, a reality and could possibly be in connection with Charlotte's disappearance, he again lost his stomach.

"No!" cried Jacob.

Unfortunately, Jacob's warning was not quick enough. As James's stomach stopped spasming, he realized why Jacob had yelled. It was not because he was dilly-dallying or getting sick with the thought of his missing sister but for reasons he was now starting to feel. There was a pinch then a burning sensation first in his foot then ankle. This sensation began to spread upward. Before he was aware, Jacob had grabbed him by the collar and was running at full tilt, dragging James behind him. It was not until he heard the splashing of water then a wet, cooling wave enveloping his body that James was back to the world around him.

"W-wh-what happened?" James stammered.

"Darkness lingers where evil has been. It will easily take an innocent without them knowing in their mind."

James had heard this before; however, he had naively dismissed it as a metaphor, never dreaming that there could be a literal meaning. As this thought passed, he realized he was once again soaked from head to toe. He drudged out of the water, feeling slightly disoriented. His vision was not as sharp, as if the world had indeed lost some of its light. James shook his head, hoping the fuzziness would dissipate soon.

"How come the darkness did not affect you? We were both in the same place together."

Jacob gave a half-grin and shrugged his shoulders. "This wood is strange and mysterious. One not knows the ways of its workings. Though luck has befallen us, for if we had both been taken, we would not be standing so strongly."

It was true that the land of the mystical creatures held many secrets, but the reason behind James's experience with darkness was not one of them. However, Jacob's resistance was one he was sworn to keep from all outsiders or else be subject to exile from the only home he had ever known. Being born a fawn, a creature that holds goodness and trickery in its soul, Jacob was unavoidably connected to the Black Shadow through ancient blood. Through this connection, any lingering poisons from the evil cannot penetrate and weaken him. If he were to divulge this information to James, not only would he be sharing the secrets of the forest with an outsider and putting its inhabitants in danger, but also James would most certainly become even more wary and distrusting of Jacob. The latter would sadden Jacob greatly for the fact that Jacob rarely came across beings he enjoyed the company of.

As the boys continued on, the sun dimmed, allowing the first of the night's stars to sparkle. It was time to find a camp and something to eat. While Jacob was scouting the area for a place to set for the night, James was impatiently ridding his face and hair of the sticky spiderweb thread that he walked directly into while looking upward at the patterned leaves of the trees. Jacob never went far when scouting and was always within shouting distance. He was about two hundred paces from where he had left James in his tangled mess when he heard voices and a faint smell of campfire. As he got closer, he was able to decipher conversation being spoken in the old language. The only ones known in the forest to still use this language as their primary speaking language was the Solero Clan. Jacob knew then at that moment that not only would he and James have a safe place to rest their heads and warm food in their bellies, but also they may just have found Charlotte. It would have been rude of him to simply walk into the clan's camp. He must be approached by one of them and then invited in to join. He knew just the ticket and scampered back to the place he had left James.

"James, James, believe it not, but I have happened upon the Solero Clan's camp. We will have a safe night's rest. I believe your sister may also be residing with them."

Without a response, James jumped off the log he had been resting and set off in the direction that Jacob had come from.

Jacob had not mentioned to James about the customs of entering one's camp. He wouldn't have to either if he knew James. As if on cue, about fifty paces from the camp, James tripped over a rock and screamed a high pitch scream as he flew through the air, landing on his face as he hit the hard earth. *Yes!* Jacob thought. His plan had worked.

There was a stir that came from the camp followed by a deep voice that called out, "Who dares walk in the night of the forest? You must be brave or dumb. If you are the former, identify yourself now, or tempt the fate of my poison arrow to your heart."

This announcement, of course, struck James dumb as he was now standing on his two feet once again. "I am Jacob the fawn, born to these woods as you. With me, I have a traveler. Pure of heart he is, no danger to you or I."

There was a rustling in the bushes to their right. Like magic, the underbrush parted, revealing a creature so magnanimous that tears began to well up in James' eyes. In a voice that seemed to silence the woods, the creature addressed them, "I am Lord Dylan, born to these woods as you, leader of the Solero Clan, hunter of the Black Shadow. What is your business so deep? These parts linger with danger not suitable for common creatures such as yourselves."

Jacob cringed at being called a common creature; in fact, his line of blood was especially rare in these times. He summarized their journey with the misfortune of its beginnings. Jacob finished with a question of Charlotte's whereabouts. The centaur did not answer and simply grabbed James, placing him on his back and turning toward the camp. Jacob followed in silence.

Upon entering the camp, light filled the forest as if it were day once again. Around the perimeter of the camp, there were campfires built, each of them for the families that made up the Solero Clan. Few of them occupied at the moment as it was still early, and feasting still abound around the largest fire that blazed at the center of the camp. There seemed to be hundreds of clansmen. All the adult males, adorned in their warrior costumes and ready for battle whenever they should meet it, were playing with their younger kin. They played at sword fighting, spear throwing, and archery competitions. This was a fun way to teach their young to become warriors.

The women were all around the camp. Some were tending the food from fire to table. Others tended the fires themselves or to the children while still, others relaxed and chitchatted with their fellow clansmen.

Jacob had heard from stories that the Solero Clan was large, though in his mind, he pictured no more than twenty or thirty total. As he looked around, however, there must have been close to one hundred clansmen and women.

James had been so caught up in the surroundings that he hadn't noticed they had come to a stop at the fire on the outermost perimeter of the camp. James knew then that he was at the fire of somebody of great power. He had studied the layouts of many warrior clans and knew that most were laid out in a spiral shape with the strongest, most seasoned warriors set on the outer perimeter for the best protection. The families with the youngest members as well as the most feeble were in the innermost section. This fire belonged to Dylan. There was, of course, the fire as well as a small leintoo shelter made from branches and leaves with a soft moss flooring. As James's eyes returned to the glow of the fire, he noticed a heap of blankets with a tuft of blonde hair poking out the side.

"*Charlotte*!" James screamed, attempting to climb down from Dylan's back. With unsuccessful grace, he misjudged the distance to the ground, falling flat on his bottom. He scrambled to stand but was stopped by Dylan's powerful hand.

"Silence, child!" Dylan said in a gruff tone that James knew to respect. "Do not disturb her. She is very weak right now. When the Black Shadow tried to take her, it drained her almost fully. She must be strong and pure of heart, for the Shadow was unsuccessful in his hunt. Good for her, but that means it is out there at the moment, still looking to fill its void that was left by your sister. With proper rest and care, she should make a full recovery, though I will warn you that those who have been touched by the Black Shadow often suffer from nightmares for many months following the incident. You may stay here until your sister is well enough to travel, and then I will guide you back to your kingdom. I will have the mother watch over your sister until that time comes. As for the two of you, go get yourselves some hot food and drink. Make yourselves at home by the fire. My people will welcome you, for they are used to travelers as we are that of the nomadic type ourselves."

Three days had passed since the night Jacob and James had entered the camp of the Solero Clan. James spent his days practicing the art of archery with the other clan novices while Jacob entertained the youngest of the clan with tales of his life in the forest. Charlotte was recovering faster than most who had been touched by the Black Shadow and lived. She was up walking around and with a good appetite. The three of them were starting to settle into a daily routine. This was an indicator to Dylan that it was about the time to guide the travelers to their destination.

That evening, Dylan approached Jacob, James, and Charlotte at the feasting fire. "We will leave at daybreak. It is then that there will be enough light to see the

Shadow coming if it is in the vicinity. It will be me and two of my men who will guide you to your kingdom. The journey should only take a day and one half."

This bit of news gave mixed feelings to all. James and Charlotte surely missed their family as well as the safety and familiarity of the kingdom, but they would also miss the friends they had made on this misadventure. Jacob was deeply saddened by the fact that in just a day and a half, he would be on his own once again.

As the fires dulled to warming coals with the clan members curled up next to them, sliding soundlessly into dream, Charlotte lay awake. Restless and unable to get comfortable, she turned to James. "James, are you awake? James?"

The only response from James was a snort, a readjustment of body position, and then the drone of a snore.

Charlotte tried to roll over into a comfortable position unsuccessfully. She could not stop thinking about this whole journey.

Charlotte woke with a jerk. As she looked around, she noticed it was still dark, but she could tell by the change in temperature the world gets just before the sun kisses the edge of the world that dawn was on the horizon. Dylan and his men were readying themselves on the other side of the fire. The day was dreary with a misty rain falling through the forest, causing the smell of wet moss and dirt to overwhelm the air. Charlotte took this moment of silent solitude to immerse herself once more in this fantastical place she ended up. What an adventure they have had to get here. She was saddened that these would be the last moments she would have of this place. Nobody from the kingdom would believe her or James about most of what they had experienced. The royal court would chalk it up to one of their shenanigans. This thought brought the wonder of how long they had actually been gone and if their family missed them.

Many of the clan gathered to see off their visitors. Some of the youngsters cried as they clung to one last hug from their new friends. The day they had ahead of them was going to be long and arduous. They set off away from camp following the ever-fading North Star. Dylan led the way, followed by Charlotte, James, and Jacob. His two men flanked the back, occasionally sweeping the area on all sides within a few kilometers of the traveling party. Nobody was particularly chatty as they walked along, each lost in their own heads, thinking about what was to come next.

The mist was heavy, making the forest floor difficult to travel. The mud and leaves on every hill created the need to skate rather than walk. The day continued dark and dreary, matching everybody's mood. They went on like this all day, only stopping for a short while to eat some lunch. It was late when they finally broke for the night. Everyone was covered up to their knees and elbows with wetness and discomfort, none of them ambitious enough to do anything other than eat before sleep. Rough shelters were built while a rustic forest stew warmed on the fire. As they sat around the fire, warming themselves inside and out, it was Dylan who broke the monotonous sound of chewing and slurping.

"We will be arriving at the perimeter of your kingdom midmorning tomorrow. As creatures of the forest, we are not permitted to enter the confines of the kingdom. It is there we will have to leave you."

"Thank you, Dylan. We know our kingdom very well, and we will be able to go straight back to our home. Both Charlotte and I appreciate everything you have done for us. You and your men saved my sister's life and allowed our friend, Jacob, and me into your camp until my sister was healed, and now are bringing us home. There is nothing we could do to repay you for this magnificent gesture of kindness."

"All I ask is that you remember this and spread the word throughout your kingdom that not all creatures of the Mystical Forest are filled with darkness. But there is something else you must remember." Dylan leaned in so it was only James in earshot. "Charlotte has been touched by the Shadow. She will appear healed and even act it but once touched, something changes deep inside that will haunt her for the rest of time. She is not to enter the forest ever again for fear that the Shadow will find her again. She may not be so lucky as to be passing my clan's path at the moment she would need us. Do not tell her so she can live the most normal life she can."

Thankfully, the darkness of the night hid James's face as it lost all color. He knew he could not tell Charlotte and not because of the reason Dylan had mentioned. He knew his sister and her thirst for adventure. He knew that if Charlotte was forbidden to enter the forest until the end of time, the only thing she would want and try to do was to get back. He looked in Charlotte's direction and was relieved she was engaged in a conversation with Jacob, not hearing what Dylan had said.

With bellies filled and dry beds waiting, all went to bed soon after eating, falling asleep quickly from exhaustion.

The forest floor had dried, and the early morning sun was peaking through the leaves as they woke to the smell of breakfast prepared by Jacob. When it was time to pack up camp, Jacob helped James snuff out the fire with a small bucket of water, giving a little chuckle as he remembered the night he first met James and Charlotte. Moods were light with conversation and laughter among the group as they set off on the last leg of their trek. James and Jacob spoke of what they would do after they parted ways.

Charlotte daydreamed of her future adventures in the forest despite the dangers she had already faced. She also held hope that once they returned, the king and queen would be so happy that they would forget about her and her brother being punished.

Dylan led the way in silence, as most guides would who were protecting royalty, as his men scouted ahead.

It was midmorning when Dylan's men came to report that the edge of the forest was just ahead. As the traveling party summited the hill, the trees thinned, and the sunlight shone brighter. Charlotte, with little regard for safety, sprinted ahead.

"Charlotte, *wait*!"

Charlotte made no inference that she had heard James, continuing at a swift speed toward the tree line.

"James, James, look at this! Berries! Berries everywhere!" Charlotte shouted back toward her travel partners as she watched them trotting toward her. "It's the berry field, James! We are just outside the kingdom. Do you think if we bring back berries, Mom and Dad won't be so mad?"

Dylan and Jacob gave a little chuckle. James rolled his eyes, knowing full well that *mad* was not the word that could describe the feelings the king and queen were sure to have.

"Oh Charlotte, we could only be so hopeful."

The four companions now stood together, looking over the field of thousands of berry-filled bushes. There was a light breeze there at the edge where the field met the forest. Off into the distance, dark clouds moved slowly toward the kingdom.

"With you returned to your kingdom, there will be sadness inside of me. Friends I did not have before will be gone and I to myself in the forest. You have shown great kindness, trust, and friendship. Thanks to you for that." Jacob looked at the sky, then he added, "A storm shall be here soon. You must be off, for the two of you would dislike greatly to be caught in the downpour. Be quick, and miss it you will."

James, who had become fond of his friendship with Jacob, felt a sadness he had not felt in his life before. It was not that of stubbing your toe or even having your feelings hurt. It was that of grief. He would grieve the departure from his friend, Jacob, knowing that neither one would be able to visit the other. He reached out and embraced Jacob in a deep hug. With his head buried in Jacob's shoulder, he muffled, "Thank you, dear friend."

There was no response from Jacob, only a small pat on James's back as a sign of recognition to the grief that would be felt by both of them upon their parting. James then turned to Dylan, giving him a strong handshake.

"I will not forget what we spoke of. Thank you again for what you have done for my sister and me. Be well, and know that you will be known as friends among our kingdom."

Charlotte gave both Dylan and Jacob a deep hug, thanking them both for saving her life while showing kindness and friendship. With goodbyes and well-beings said, the two siblings set off into the berry field in hopes to make it home before the storm broke the skies. Taking no time to reach the other side, they stepped onto the path.

James noticed a pile of brush that was in disarray.

"Hey, Charlotte, I think this is where I crashed before we got lost in the forest."

James turned back toward the field where Charlotte had stopped at the edge to pick a few berries in happiness before facing the unknown of her parents. She wasn't there! With panic in his voice, he called out for her.

"Charlotte! Charlotte! *Where are you?*"

There was a rustling from the bushes where James was looking at instead of the field he had just left.

"What are you hollering for, James? I'm right here, you goose." Charlotte stepped out onto the path with a mouthful of raspberries. "What is the matter?"

"It's gone, Charlotte! It's not there! Look!"

"James, what *are* you talking about?"

"The field! It disappeared."

Charlotte turned and saw just that bushes James was looking at. The field she and her brother had just stepped from, the one that held the berries that now stained her face, was gone and replaced by trees and underbrush.

"*Whoa*, so cool! So it is true. I thought Obryn was teasing me."

"What do you mean?

"Obryn said that when Mom and Dad punish someone in the kingdom, they are cut off from the berry field until they are pardoned of the punishment. But she never mentioned being blasted to the Mystical Forest."

James stood there with a bewildered look upon his face as he listened to Charlotte.

"Oh shoot!"

"What? What's wrong?"

"We can't see the field."

"Right. Don't you think you have had enough? By the looks of your face, you are going to have a stomachache."

"No, James, that's not it. Don't you see? If we cannot see the field, that means Mom and Dad are still mad!" She slumped her shoulders and stomped her foot. "Harrumph! You would *think* after days of us missing, they would have forgiven the mishap at the market. Man, can they hold a grudge."

Though James thought this peculiar, he shrugged his shoulders with indifference. A boom sounded from the sky at that moment, making both of them jump.

"Come on, Charlotte! Let's get home before the storm hits."

Looking up, the clouds had begun to thicken, and the sky darkened. There was another boom of thunder.

"Last one home is a drowned rat!"

"Wait, what?"

Before James could comprehend, Charlotte took off at top-flight speed. James followed, weaving in and out of branches, trying desperately to pass Charlotte. But she had gotten a head start due to the element of surprise. Charlotte kept the lead all the way to the scullery door.

"Where in the holy forest have you two been? It has been hours since you were sent for berries, yet you return with none."

James and Charlotte looked at each other, confused. *Hours? Try days.*

"And don't even think about lying to me. The evidence is all over your face, little miss."

Charlotte opened her mouth to speak but was interrupted.

"The house will go without muffins tomorrow morning, and there certainly can't be any pies baked for this evening's meal without berries. What do you two have to say for yourselves?"

It was James who attempted to speak this time, but he was also interrupted by the head scullery maid.

"You know what, never you mind. Just *wait* until your parents hear about you two skipping out on your day of chores. They will be none too happy, you know."

The thunder boomed, the lightning cracked, and the sky opened up.

"You two get back to your rooms until dinner. Make sure to wash up now. Both of you look like you had quite the adventure today."

James and Charlotte both smirked at this comment.

"Oh, children, I wouldn't be smiling if I were you. Now go! Get on with you!"

It was a quiet dinner that evening. James and Charlotte had been scolded once again with more restrictions put in place for a length of time that was undetermined. Neither one of them ever explained what really happened. If they had, it would sure to have been viewed as lies with further punishment to follow. In their silence they finished dinner and headed to bed. Exhaustion, from their time on their misadventure, took them quickly to sleep.

Charlotte was running through the mystical forest, screaming with no sound coming from within her. She was screaming her bother's name. As she ran, her vision got blurrier and blurrier until...

Charlotte woke with a start with sweat covering her body.

About the Author

M. R. Myers was born and raised in New Hampshire. Her passion for teaching stemmed from an early age. M. R. Myers has taught in the classroom as well as among the equine world. After working with children with special needs, she went on and obtained her associate's degree in early childhood education in 2011. From there, she moved to Virginia and worked in a Montessori school with elementary-aged children. Taking a break from the teaching field, she moved back to New Hampshire, where she currently resides with her dog.

CPSIA information can be obtained
at www.ICGtesting.com
Printed in the USA
BVHW021059241121
622430BV00011B/222/J

9 781639 851584